BIG!

tim hopgood

Picture Corgi

For ROSY, PAUL, FREDDIE, SAMUEL & LEO

BIG!
A PICTURE CORGI BOOK 978 0 552 56487 8

Published in Great Britain by Picture Corgi, an imprint of Random House Children's Publishers UK
A Random House Group Company
This edition published 2013

1 3 5 7 9 10 8 6 4 2

Copyright © Tim Hopgood, 2013
The right of Tim Hopgood to be identified as the author and illustrator of this work has been asserted in accordance with the Copyright, Designs and Patents Act 1988. All rights reserved. No part of this publication may be reproduced, stored in a retrieval system, or transmitted in any form or by any means, electronic, mechanical, photocopying, recording or otherwise, without the prior permission of the publishers.

Picture Corgi Books are published by Random House Children's Publishers UK, 61–63 Uxbridge Road, London W5 5SA
www.**randomhousechildrens**.co.uk www.**randomhouse**.co.uk
Addresses for companies within The Random House Group Limited can be found at: www.randomhouse.co.uk/offices.htm
THE RANDOM HOUSE GROUP Limited Reg. No. 954009
A CIP catalogue record for this book is available from the British Library.
Printed in China

The Random House Group Limited supports the Forest Stewardship Council®(FSC®), the leading international forest certification organisation. Our books carrying the FSC label are printed on FSC®-certified paper. FSC is the only forest certification scheme endorsed by the leading environmental organisations, including Greenpeace. Our paper procurement policy can be found at www.randomhouse.co.uk/environment.

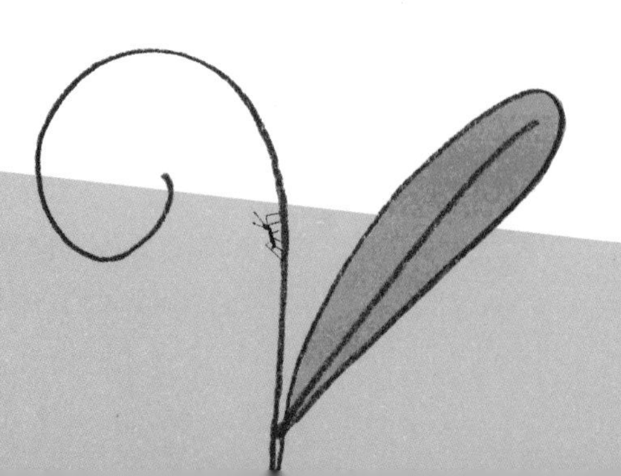

(I don't know.)

I can touch my toes,

but I can't
touch the sky.

Standing next to my friend BIG Ben
I'm just little me, but . . .

I'm growing.

I'M BIGGER

than I used to be
I know that for sure.

**I can see
my face in the
bathroom mirror.**

But when will I be
BIG?

Next to an ant, I'm a
GINORMOUS
GIANT.

next to a bear,

I'm really quite small.

I'm growing.
I know
I am.

My trousers don't reach down to my ankles anymore.

But when will I be

BIG?

Next to a popcorn I'm

MASSIVE.

I must be
at least
500
popcorns
tall.

BUT
next to these buildings,

I'm
really
quite
small.

I'M SURE I'M GETTING
LONGER.

I can feel the end of my bed
with my toes.

Compared with a mouse I'm
GIGANTIC

But compared with an elephant,
I'm a titch.

I'M GROWING.

I know I am.

I can now reach the light-switch

to turn

ON

the light.

BUT I WONDER,
WHEN WILL I BE

BIG?

I'M GROWING.

I know I am.

Here's all the

PROOF

I need –

for the

first time

ever

I'm a tiny bit

taller than

my friend

BIG

BEN.

Me JULY

Ben JULY

Ben JUNE

Ben MAY

Me JUNE

Ben APRIL

Ben MARCH

Ben FEB

Me MAY

Me APRIL

Ben JAN

Me MARCH

Me FEB

Me JAN

Now I know I'm

BIG!

And
one
day . . .

I'll be even **BIGGER** than Dad . . .

and that's as

BIG

as

BIG

can be!